Race Ahead with Reading

The Big Bad Wolf and the Robot Pig

By Laura North

Illustrated by Kevin Cross

Crabtree Publishing Company
www.crabtreebooks.com

Crabtree Publishing Company
www.crabtreebooks.com
1-800-387-7650

616 Welland Ave.   PMB 59051, 350 Fifth Ave.
St. Catharines, ON   59th Floor,
L2M 5V6   New York, NY 10118

Published by Crabtree Publishing Company in 2015

First published in 2012 by Franklin Watts
(A division of Hachette Children's Books)

Text © Laura North 2012
Illustration © Kevin Cross 2012

Series editor: Melanie Palmer
Series advisor: Catherine Glavina
Series designer: Peter Scoulding
Editor: Kathy Middleton
**Proofreader and
   notes to adults:** Shannon Welbourn
**Production coordinator and
   Prepress technician:** Ken Wright
Print coordinator: Katherine Berti

Printed in Hong Kong/082014/BK20140613

**Library and Archives Canada
Cataloguing in Publication**

CIP available at Library and Archives Canada

**Library of Congress
Cataloging-in-Publication Data**

North, Laura.
  The big bad wolf and the robot pig / by Laura
North ; illustrated by Kevin Cross.
     pages cm. -- (Race ahead with reading)
  "First published in 2012 by Franklin Watts"--
Copyright page.
  ISBN 978-0-7787-1291-6 (reinforced library binding)
-- ISBN 978-0-7787-1362-3 (pbk.) --
ISBN 978-1-4271-7781-0 (electronic pdf) --
ISBN 978-1-4271-7769-8 (electronic html)
[1. Wolves--Fiction. 2. Pigs--Fiction. 3. Robots--
Fiction. 4. Humorous stories.] I. Cross, Kevin,
illustrator. II. Title.

  PZ7.N8144Bi 2014
  [E]--dc23
                                    2014020696

Chapter 1

"I'll huff, and I'll puff, and I'll blow your house down!" cried the Wolf.

"Huff!

Puff!

Huff! Puff! Huff..."

"You can't get us, Mr. Wolf!"
squealed the Three Little Pigs.
"You're hairy and scary.
But we're too clever for you!"

However, only one of the
pigs was actually clever.

One pig was very lazy.

The third was very greedy.

Clever Pig had knocked down the houses made of straw and wood. He built all their new houses from strong steel, with hi-tech security systems.

"Huff…

   Puff…

      Wheeze!"

The Wolf huffed and puffed until he was

panting out of breath. "I give up," he said.

He walked away with his tail

between his legs.

That evening, he sat at his
dinner table with nothing to eat.
"I can't scare the pigs any more.
That means no more bacon,
sausages, or ham."

Just the thought of the juicy
meat made the Wolf hungrier. He licked
his lips. "I have to get those pigs!"

Suddenly, the Wolf had an idea.

Chapter 2

"If I can't get into the pigs' houses," said the Wolf, "I will make them come to me!"

The Wolf got to work at once. He hammered and banged, and sparks flew everywhere! He used tin cans and an egg carton.

He worked all night until, finally,
his creation was ready.

"I will call him Robot Pig,"
said the Wolf.

"Robot Pig will knock on the Three Little Pigs' doors and invite them to a dinner party at my house. He will be the perfect trap." laughed the Wolf.

"Hmm... he doesn't look much like a pig," the Wolf worried.

"I know!" he cried. He went to the cupboard and got out a big tin of pink paint.
"This will do the trick," he said, pouring paint all over the metal creature.

Then the Wolf got out a remote control and pressed a big red button.

"Oink!" said the Pig. "Hello, Master!"

"Eureka!" shouted the Wolf.
"It works!"

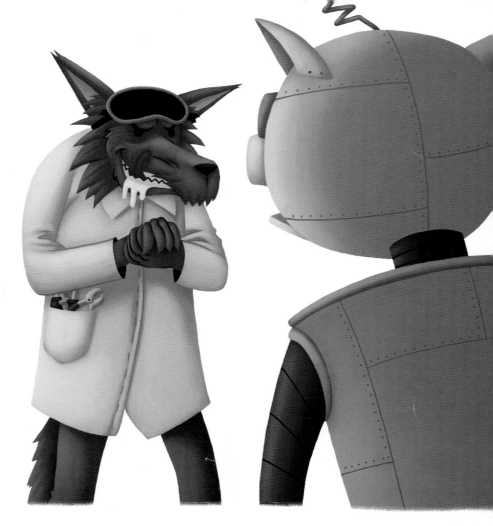

The Wolf looked hungrily at the Robot Pig.

"If you weren't made out of tin cans,

I would eat you all up."

He smiled, licking his lips.

Chapter 3

"Zzzzz…" Lazy Pig was having a nap when there was a knock at his door.

"Who is it?" asked Lazy Pig sleepily.

"I am your new neighbor," said Robot Pig.

"Phew, it's just a big pig! I thought it might be the Wolf trying to eat me," sighed Lazy Pig.

He slid the door chains off and unlocked the deadbolts. The door swung open.

"Hello," said the Robot Pig.

"I would like to invite you

to a dinner party this evening."

"Oh," yawned Lazy Pig.

"I really do have a lot of sleeping to do."

"There will be a big bed full of

soft straw and fluffy pillows,"

added Robot Pig.

"In that case, count me in!"

said Lazy Pig.

Next, Robot Pig knocked at the door

of Greedy Pig.

"Hello. Please come to my party.

There will be huge plates of cakes, jello,

ice cream, and milkshakes."

"Yes, yes, yes!" said Greedy Pig, drooling.
"I'll be there!"

"My plan is working perfectly!" whispered
the Wolf, peering out from behind a bush.

Finally, Robot Pig knocked on
the door of Clever Pig's house.
"We are holding a dinner party for all
the cleverest pigs in the country.
Will you be our guest of honor?"

Clever Pig was easily flattered.
"Of course!" he said proudly.

The Wolf smiled, flashing two rows of pointy, yellow teeth.

"What a feast I will have—tasty pigs as the appetizer, main course, and dessert!"

Chapter 4

Knock! Knock! Knock!

The Wolf heard the sound of hoofs tapping

on his door. Three juicy pigs were outside.

"I don't need to go out for dinner,"

said the Wolf, "I've got room service."

The Wolf hid behind the cupboard.

Using the remote control, he rolled

Robot Pig to the front door.

"Welcome to my dinner party,"
said Robot Pig. "Do come in."
There was one big, empty plate in the
middle of the table.

"Where's the bed?" asked Lazy Pig.

"Where's the food?" asked Greedy Pig.

"Where are all the clever pigs?"
asked Clever Pig.

"Have something to eat," said Robot Pig.

The Clever Pig looked more closely
at Robot Pig.

"You're only painted pink!" he said.

"We've been tricked!"

"Yes," said the Wolf as he jumped out

from behind the cupboard.

"It's time for my dinner!"

He chased them around the table.

"Squeal!" cried the pigs.

Chapter Five

The Wolf was just about take a big bite out of Greedy Pig when Clever Pig noticed something.

"The Wolf left the remote control by the front door," he thought.

He picked it up and pressed the big red button in the middle.

"OINK! OINK! OINK!" said Robot Pig.

Clever Pig pushed the lever forward.

Robot Pig rolled toward the Wolf.

"What's happening?" the Wolf cried.

"OINK! OINK! OINK!"

roared Robot Pig.

The Wolf looked up in terror.

"Stop!" he cried.

"I'm your master, remember?"

"You're hairy and scary,"
said Robot Pig.

"Argggh!" screamed the Wolf,
and he ran out of the house.

Robot Pig whizzed after him
on his super-fast robo wheels.

"That Robot Pig saved our bacon,"

said Greedy Pig.

"This is a nice house, isn't it?"

said Clever Pig.

"Yes," said Lazy Pig.

"We could be very comfortable here."

Outside, Robot Pig chased the Wolf
over the hills and out of the village,
never to return.

Notes for Adults

These entertaining, first chapter books help children build up their reading skills so they can move on to longer books. Fun illustrations and bite-sized chapters encourage young readers to take the driver's seat and *Race Ahead with Reading.*

THE FOLLOWING BEFORE, DURING, AND AFTER READING ACTIVITY SUGGESTIONS SUPPORT LITERACY SKILL DEVELOPMENT AND CAN ENRICH SHARED READING EXPERIENCES:

BEFORE

1. Make reading fun! Choose a time to read when you and the reader are relaxed and have time to share the story together. Don't forget to give praise! Children learn best in a positive environment.
2. Before reading, ask the reader to look at the title and illustration on the cover of the book **The Big Bad Wolf and the Robot Pig**. Invite them to make predictions about what will happen in the story. They may make use of prior knowledge and make connections to other stories they have heard or read about the Big Bad Wolf or another similar character.

DURING

3. Encourage readers to determine unfamiliar words themselves by using clues from the text and illustrations.
4. During reading, encourage the child to review his or her understanding and see if they want to revise their predictions midway. Encourage the reader to make text-to-text connections, choosing a part of the story that reminds them of another story they have read; and text-to-self connections, choosing a part of the story that relates to their own personal experiences; and text-to-world connections, choosing a part of the story that reminds them of something that happened in the real world.

AFTER

5. Ask the reader **who** the main characters are in this story. Have the child **retell** the story in their own words. Ask him or her to think about the predictions they made before reading the story. How were they the same or different?

DISCUSSION QUESTIONS FOR KIDS

6. Throughout this story, the Big Bad Wolf is presented with problems. What does he do to solve the problems he faces?
7. Choose one of the illustrations from the story. How do the details in the picture help you to understand a part of the story better? Or, what do they tell you that is not in the text?
8. The Big Bad Wolf uses the Robot Pig to trick the pigs. Have you ever been tricked? What happened?
9. Have you ever tricked someone? How did you feel about what you did? Was it a good or bad decision? Explain.
10. Which character in this story do you relate to most? Why?
11. Create your own story or drawing about a problem or challenge you had and how you solved it.